Knight of the Jungle

ARI CUMBUSYAN

DEDICATION

I dedicate this book to my family. To every single one of you, thank you for all the things you've done for me.

CONTENTS

Acknowledgments   i

1   A Warm Welcome   Pg 1

2   Stuck in a Cage   Pg 7

3   Guards, Guards and more Guards   Pg 13

4   The Dungeon of Puzzles   Pg 21

5   The War Begins   Pg 32

6   A New Beginning   Pg 39

7   The Important Fruit   Pg 55

Epilogue   Pg 63

ACKNOWLEDGMENTS

I would like to thank my mother and father for helping me edit this story to make it what it is now, and my teachers, Ms Hugo and Ms Tracy for encouraging me and helping me publish this book.

.

1. A WARM WELCOME

Malcolm was tired. The Amazon Rainforest was a harsh, unforgiving place, and he was learning that the hard way. His boots were making his feet hurt, and his chest plate was so uncomfortable that he was thinking about throwing it away. He dismissed this idea, as he reminded himself that the armour kept him safe. The gash on his shoulder from his fight with the bandits made him want to kill Ervarath, the evil warlord, more than ever. He trudged through the jungle, using his sword to cut through the foliage. Each swing tore his shoulder wound open more and more. He ignored the pain. "I will eventually find the village," he told himself. He hoped the village would be close, but the mapping of the regions he was in were vague. For all he knew, the village could be miles away, in which case he would bleed to death.

Malcolm had set out as a young knight, to try to kill Ervarath and make these regions safe again. The exotic fruits and spices from South America went for a high price back in Europe, and England wanted to make the first move. Every big European nation was competing for control of the South American countries, and with that, to gain control of the spice trade. England had missed out on Africa and this was their last chance on big money. Malcolm had been picked to eliminate Ervarath, so that England could send ships to begin the operation to extract expensive items that could be brought back to England and sold. Even though Malcolm was still young and had been trying to kill Ervarath for only two months, he felt like an old man. His long, brown hair got caught in a branch and he cursed, and untangled it. As he trudged on, the hot, unforgiving sun slowly roasting his back, he dragged himself through the jungle, concentrating on putting one foot in front of the other. The forest got darker and darker, and eventually, Malcolm settled down to sleep. He hated sleeping in the jungle. The noises that he heard made him afraid, and he longed for his comfortable bed in the castle back home. He pitched his tent, and eventually fell into a light sleep.

The next morning, Malcolm packed up his things and set off. The top of the sun poked up over the horizon, basking the jungle in a pale yellow. After about an hour, he smelled meat cooking, and heard a faint song. He began to drool, but slapped himself. "I'm going insane," he muttered. He decided to give himself a quick pep talk. "You, Malcolm, are a great knight. You shall kill the evil Ervarath, and proudly serve your country!" He looked down at his feet and focused on making small steps, pretending the ache in his feet wasn't there. After a while, he stopped and looked around. On his left was a dirty brick path, leading into the thick jungle. He followed it excitedly. Surely this would lead to the village! He went around a corner and the village burst into view. He ran towards it, feeling like someone had just poured pure energy and elation all over him. He saw a wonderful scene, as if from a dream, and his senses thanked him for being there at that moment in time. The scent of food and exotic spices greeted his nose, and he could almost taste them in his mouth. The smell, not pungent in any way, was gentle, almost like a mother caressing her children, and was balanced, it seemed, almost perfectly. His eyes were greeted with bright colors, and the clothing of the village people stunned him. The dresses of the women swirled and flowed like waves as they danced, and the shirts of the men were also covered in vibrant colors.

Malcolm laid down his sword, and a man, who Malcolm assumed was the village leader, walked up to him.

"Welcome!" He smiled. He had a slight, almost imperceptible accent, but nevertheless seemed to speak English perfectly. Most natives could speak English, as most of the Europeans who had tried to come here for spices in the first place had learned basic English as a common language. "I see you come in peace!" He continued, and Malcolm nodded. "My name is Luis. What is yours?"

"Malcolm," He replied.

"It is very nice to meet you." Luis said. He noticed Malcolm's shoulder injury and gasped. "Ay-ay-ay!" He exclaimed. "What has happened to your shoulder?" He looked genuinely concerned.

"Nothing much, just a fight with some bandits that didn't go as planned." Malcolm replied.

"But we must heal this wound at once! Those bandits are nothing but trouble." Luis said, while two men left the area. They returned with an old leather bag, and handed it to Luis. "Thank you," Luis told the men.

"Anytime," they chorused. A woman walked up to Luis and took the bag. She had long, black hair that went down to her shoulders, bright blue eyes, and a small nose, with high cheekbones. She was wearing a tool belt of sorts, a long, colorful dress, and a green jacket with many pockets. She looked about thirty years old.

"This is Rafaela, the village healer," Said Luis. Rafaela opened the bag and pulled out a bottle filled with a thick green, liquid, and some bandages. Then she took out a bottle filled with a clear liquid, a bottle filled with a yellow liquid, and a syringe.

4

"This will clean the wound," Rafaela said, pointing to the clear liquid. "This will ease the pain," She continued, pointing to the yellow liquid. "This is a salve which will help the wound to heal," She finished, pointing to the thick, green liquid. She took out an incredibly thin strand and a needle. "I am assuming you are alright with this?" Luis asked.

"Yes, of course," Malcolm said. He felt a strange trust for these people. Although he had only just got there, he felt like he knew the village and its people well.

"You may take him away," Luis said. Rafaela brought Malcolm into a small, red house. Inside, there was a mattress on the floor.

"Lie down," Rafaela said. Malcolm did as she asked. Malcolm took off his chest plate, chainmail, and tunic. Rafaela filled the syringe with the yellow liquid, the anesthetic. Then she poured some of the clear liquid, the disinfectant, onto a clean, white piece of cloth, and rubbed the cloth around the tip of the syringe. "We are ready," She announced. She poked the syringe into Malcolm's arm. He felt a slight sting, and then fell into a deep sleep.

When he woke up, Malcolm was still on the mattress. Rafaela was standing next to him. "I see you are awake," She said. "Look at your shoulder," The cut was all patched up, and bandaged.

"Thank you!" Malcolm exclaimed, gratefully.

"No problem," Rafaela replied, though the hint of a smile showed on her face. "You must drink," She said, and picked up a flask. Malcolm realized how thirsty he was. Rafaela helped him pour some of the water into his mouth and he gulped it down, gratefully. "Too much, too fast is not good for you," Rafaela said, then put her finger on a spot on Malcolm's neck. "Pulse is good," Rafaela reported. "Come on," She said. "You need rest. There is a room waiting for you."

Malcolm stepped into the room, and saw a bed with a blue blanket, a bamboo pipe that went into the wall with some space above it, and a stool. There was also a big window with embroidered curtains.

"Push down the pipe for water," Rafaela instructed. Malcolm pushed down the pipe, and fresh, cold, water, flowed out. The water fell into a bucket on the floor with a splash. "The water here is drinkable," Rafaela said. "Go on, drink if you are thirsty, but not too fast," Malcolm turned the tap on, and put his mouth under the flowing water. It tasted pure, as if an entire freshwater lake had been poured into his mouth. Malcolm wiped his mouth with the back of his hand and walked over to the bed. He took off his leather boots, lay down on the bed, and for the second time that day, fell into a deep sleep.

2. STUCK IN A CAGE

Malcolm stayed in the village for a few more days, spending most of his time resting and thinking about what he was to do next. However, eventually the time came for him to leave. He took food and water, and thanked the villagers profusely for their help. Then, he set off, vowing to repay the village people somehow if he returned. When he returned, he corrected himself. It began to rain, and Malcolm slipped on a tree root. He stood up, and as he was dusting himself off, an arrow bounced off his chest plate. Malcolm was surprised, but being a knight, he had been trained for these kinds of moments. He drew his sword from his sheath, and it made a metallic ring, as if to show it was hungry for blood. He ran over to a gigantic tree and saw three bowmen. He lunged with his sword and impaled one. The bowman looked at his chest for a second, with an

7

almost confused look on his face. Why did you do this? The look seemed to say. Malcolm spun around and sliced into another man. The man screamed in agony and fell to the ground, writhing. Then Malcolm ducked an attempt to be struck by a dagger, as the bowmen carried these. The last bowman had enough time to get a hold of something else to defend himself with. Malcolm faked a side cut, then quick as lightning, hacked into the man's neck, with all of his strength. The man's body fell to the floor. The head wasn't attached to it. Instead, it flew through the air before hitting the trunk of a tree with a sickening crunch. Malcolm tried to step over the body, but another man appeared in front of him and shoved him back. Malcolm fell and found himself in a cage. The man quickly slammed the cage door shut and locked it.

"A fighter, eh?" The man said. He had a thick brown mustache, and a voice like a raspy crow. Malcolm said nothing. "Take him away," The man said.

The bandit village was in a large clearing, and the lush, green trees around the clearing stood strong and tall, and a tree frog hopped up the branches. The village was warm because of a big bonfire in the center. Sparks flew up into the air, and as the flames danced, Malcolm sadly reflected that if he had been on the same side as the bandits, he might have been enjoying himself. Instead, he was stuck here, in this stupid cage. The cage was suspended by a rope on the edge of a tree branch. The bandits had assigned a guard to make sure Malcolm didn't get away. Malcolm smelled the food, and his nose would have grinned if it had a face. The smell of fish from the Amazon river slowly being cooked to perfection was too much for Malcolm, and his stomach growled. The guard heard him and smirked.

"You hungry?" He asked. He had messy, curly brown hair, broad shoulders, olive skin, and sparkling green eyes.

"Yes," Malcolm replied, rather annoyed.

"You will get a meal tomorrow," He replied, as if sensing Malcolm's annoyance. "My name is Daniel,"

"Mine is Malcolm," said Malcolm. All of a sudden, a big, burly man ran over to them. "Daniel! What have I said about talking to the prisoners?" The man said, glaring at Malcolm accusingly. Malcolm felt like the man's eyes were boring into him, and he felt very uncomfortable. "If you say anything to my son, I will personally rip you apart. Understood?"

"Yes, sir," Malcolm whispered. He was in no position to disobey orders. Aside from that, he had a very strong feeling that the man would actually rip him apart. He shivered. The man muttered something under his breath and walked away. Malcolm vowed that if he escaped, he would make this man pay. When he escaped, he corrected himself. When he escaped.

Daniel kept talking to Malcolm the next morning.

"I love my father, but I think he is too overprotective,"
Daniel said. Malcolm asked why, and Daniel's face darkened. "My sister," he said. "She died. We don't talk about her," He finished, fighting back tears. They sat in silence, sweat running down their backs. The sun was especially hot, and Malcolm had sunburn. At noon, his meal, some fish and plantain, was given to him. It was extremely simple, yet Malcolm had never tasted anything that good. The fish was light and yet succulent, and the plantain, which tasted similar to a potato, was sort of creamy and yet sweet. As Malcolm wolfed the food down, he had an idea. It was ambitious, and it would be difficult, but if he pulled it off, he would be able to escape, and he might just be able to defeat Ervarath as well.

"Why do you guys work with Ervarath?" Malcolm asked innocently, on the fourth day of his time as a prisoner.
"We're not the only ones!" Daniel replied, defensively.
"Yes, I know, but, why do you work with him?" Malcolm asked again. Daniel took a deep breath, and began.
"Ervarath saved my father's life. No one knows why. My father's evil brother tried to throw him off a cliff. As my thirty year old dad hung on to the edge of the cliff with one hand, He began to slip. As his last finger began to slide off, Ervarath caught him. Don't

ask me why. I don't know why my father and Ervarath were even traveling with each other. I don't know the details of the situation, basically." Daniel admitted. "However, I can tell you why Ervarath is doing what he is doing. You know, stealing from travelers, hurting people, and making these regions unsafe?" Malcolm nodded, not sure how to reply. "Well, the story goes that my father's brother was cursed as a child, cursed with hate. He has random outbursts of pure hate, and desire to kill the unlucky soul who he hates. Ervarath is friends with the brother, and Ervarath is trying to gather resources and other things, to lift the curse so that his friend can be normal and live a happy life. But we do have one justifiable reason as to why we are working with Ervarath. We, our clan, our village, value life, whether that be human life, the life of a snake, or even the life of a plant or insect, above all other things, although we acknowledge that natural death, without disease, is a peaceful one. This is also why our clan is very good at healing. We have gone to the ends of the Earth, and back, to stop pain, and disease. Anyway," Daniel continued, clearing his throat. "The brother has nearly killed himself on a few occasions. Some were attempted suicide because he had tried to kill his loved ones, and felt remorse after his anger went away. Others were because he nearly died trying to kill. There is no question that he will die, painfully, very soon. In fact, it is a miracle that he hasn't died already. But, Ervarath has been trying to gather things

11

he needs to lift the curse. Furthermore, he has almost all the things he needs. One of the things he needs is a true enemy's death. You are a perfect candidate." Daniel explained.

"Wait, why?" Malcolm asked.

"Think about it. Your sole purpose on your mission, or quest, or whatever it is, is to defeat Ervarath and also, stop his attempts to try to save his friend. You are the definition of his true enemy." Malcolm nodded, but then realized something. "Killing people to save one man won't save lives! It will save one while many others will die!" Malcolm argued.

"That's where you're wrong. Daniel replied. "Ervarath threatened to burn the entire forest if we do not cooperate. His base is built on a large area of rock. He is immune to fire! Almost all life in the entire forest would die, painfully, if we fail to partner with Ervarath, that is. We are working with Ervarath to protect the forest and everything in it. They stayed silent for a while, thinking about what to do.

"Haven't you thought about rebelling?" Malcolm asked.

"How would we go about doing that?" Daniel said, looking up at Malcolm in his cage.

"Well, you have the numbers. You just need to work together," replied Malcolm.

"It probably won't happen, you know that, right? It's taking a lot of self control to not call you crazy," Daniel complained.

"But can you please try?" Malcolm asked.

"Look, I'm not ruling it out. That's all I'm gonna say." Daniel replied.

3. GUARDS, GUARDS AND MORE GUARDS

It had been three days since the long conversation with Daniel about Ervarath, and Malcolm lifted himself up from his cage, which rattled and shook in protest. He still wasn't used to the way it dangled off the tree from a single rope, and his back ached after the nights on the cold, hard, metal. He groaned. *If only I was back home. Why did I even volunteer for this?* He asked himself. A deep, booming voice suddenly interrupted his thoughts. He looked up and saw Daniel's father. He was standing in front of a large crowd. "Hello, and welcome to the Vote. As you may have heard, we, as our clan, are going to vote about whether we should rebel against Ervarath. Malcolm scanned the crowd, looking for Daniel. Sure enough, he found him. They made eye contact and Daniel winked. Malcolm grinned back. Put your leaves in the containers. Red leaf means no rebellion. Green leaf means you support the rebellion. You may start. Everyone shuffled towards the boxes and dropped in their leaves. "Did you vote green?" Malcolm asked excitedly from the inside of his cage. "Of course." Daniel replied.

"Who do you think will win?"

"I can't say, though it looks like it'll be close." Daniel said.

"When will the results be announced?"

"Maybe tomorrow."

"Oh."

The Sun rose higher and higher, brightening everything up.

"Here. Take these," Daniel said, rolling something up and pushing it through a hole in the cage. Malcolm unrolled the object and saw two banana leaves.

"Put them on the bottom of your cage. Hopefully it will make your sleep more comfortable. I will try to bring more later." Daniel said.

"Thank you!" Malcolm said.

"No problem," Daniel replied, before leaving the area.

The next night was a whole lot more comfortable for Malcolm.

"Hello, everyone, and welcome to The Vote!" were the sounds that woke Malcolm up a couple of days later. Malcolm blinked and rubbed the sleep out of his eyes. By this point, the sight of Malcolm in his hanging cage was a now familiar sight to the bandits. "Hopefully everyone is doing well." Daniel's father said. "I won't wait. Here are the results of the vote." He took a deep breath, and continued. "So. The amount of votes supporting the rebellion is… 583. The number of people not supporting the rebellion is…" He frowned, and everyone held their breath. "583. A draw."

Malcolm sighed, wondering what was to be done. How would he get out of this mess? Was it his destiny to stay in a cage for the rest of his life? He looked at the jungle ground, and suddenly, an idea came to him. "Can I vote?" Malcolm asked Daniel. Daniel hesitated.

"There is a way. It is… difficult, but can be done." Daniel replied, picking his words slowly and with care.

"How?" Malcolm asked eagerly.

"I am not guaranteeing anything, however, there is a blue gem on the top of a mountain. It can heal anyone from almost any disease, sickness, or injury. If you could get a hold of it, you might be able to vote. There is one problem, though. The adventure you will have to embark upon will be dangerous, and there is a good chance you will die. And how we will we get you out of here?"

"Well, we will have to sneak me out." Malcolm replied.

"We?" Daniel asked.

The night sky was pitch black. A cold breeze blew through the air, making the trees rustle. Malcolm wondered why they hadn't thought of this before. It seemed to him that nothing could go wrong. Daniel had snuck into his father's room and stolen the keys to the cage. He opened the cage, and Malcolm hopped silently down to the ground. His legs ached from days of being inactive, and they screamed in agony. If he hadn't been trained for years to remain silent, he might have collapsed right there and then. But it didn't matter. He was free!

"Quick! We must get to the armory!" Daniel's panicked voice interrupted Malcolm's thoughts.

"Trust me, the security in our village is some of the best there is. I should also mention that if I get caught, I'm dead," Daniel hissed. They ran to the armory, a small hut near the middle of the village. Daniel opened the door and took a small, simple dagger, then went to the corner of the hut and took two brown bags. "Find your sword." Daniel said. Malcolm scanned the armory, and his eyes soon found his sword. He grabbed it, and ran out the door. The plan was going to work perfectly. It seemed there was no security after all. It was too good to be true. A heavily built man jumped out at Malcolm and tried to bring him down, but Malcolm spun away from him and kept on running. Daniel wasn't so lucky. A guard ran up from behind him.

"Watch out!" Malcolm yelled. Daniel turned, but it was too late. The guard tackled Daniel, and Malcolm turned around to face the guard. He wouldn't let his friend be caught.

"Keep going!" Daniel screamed.

"No!" Malcolm replied. "I won't leave you behind!" He leaped up into the air, and the guard realized what was about to happen to him. Malcolm stabbed the guard, who gasped in pain, then fell over on his side. Malcolm yanked his sword out and put it in his sheath.

"Come on," he said to Daniel. Daniel picked himself up and ran.

"I'll lead the way!" He panted, as they navigated around the rainforest. Eventually, they came to a small hill.

"This is it." Daniel announced.

"This small hill?" Malcolm asked, incredulously.

"Yes." Daniel replied. "Just follow me." He cleared away some vines, which revealed an old wooden door in the side of the hill. They opened the door and closed it behind them. Daniel walked up to an emerald embedded in the wall and touched it with his hand. He muttered an incantation, and the emerald glowed. "I suppose I should explain this to you." He said. "The mountain has been put under a spell, so that to anyone who doesn't follow the procedure of touching the emerald and saying the incantation, the mountain is invisible. I was going to leave you some parchment with instructions, but I suppose you won't need that now that I am here. Anyway, enough talking." He explained. They walked on until they got to another door. Daniel recited the incantation once more, and then he opened the door.

What stood before them was a mountain so gigantic, that it reached into the clouds. "It's going to be a long climb." Malcolm said.

"Looks like it." Daniel replied.

They began their long hike up the mountain on a small outcrop, about one meter wide. Malcolm was too tired to speak. He just focused on the job at hand, edging forward, to the top. However, there were no particularly dangerous threats, as far as Malcolm could see. In fact, the journey was going quite smoothly until they heard a terrifying shriek. Three red goblins with one eye each and a mouth full of razor sharp fangs dropped down onto the outcrop. "Ervarath's minions." Daniel whispered. "I should have known they would be here." He cursed. They looked at each other, and Daniel drew his dagger, before sliding under the legs of one minion, turning around and stabbing him in the back of the neck, all in one, fluid motion. Then, Malcolm lunged at one goblin, impaling him, and one goblin was left standing. It screamed in fury, and leaped up in the air, its jaws of death at the ready. Daniel kicked the goblin in the side of its stomach. The kick was strong, and the force of it pushed the goblin off the mountain.

"Wow," Malcolm said, as a bead of sweat rolled down his cheek. Daniel grinned.

"We make a good team!" Malcolm exclaimed.

"We do. These guys won't be bothering us again!" Daniel replied, happily.

There were no trees to provide shade from the sun, and Malcolm and Daniel were exposed to the blistering heat. "You could fill a lake with all of our sweat!" Malcolm joked, a few hours after the fight with the minions.

"That's disgusting." Daniel replied, although he smiled when he said it. There was a grinding noise from deep inside the mountain, and a wooden log with a cage attached to a rope popped out of the side of the mountain. The cage came crashing down on them, and Malcolm immediately tried to lift up the bottom of the cage. It was stuck.

"I hate cages." Malcolm grumbled.

Malcolm and Daniel decided to use their weapons to cut through the cage. The second Daniel started his attempt to cut through the cage, the floor inside the cage began to rise. They worked harder and faster, until they eventually cut through the cage. "Quick!" Daniel shouted. Malcolm leaped out. Daniel tried to follow, but his shoe got caught between the top of the cage and the floor. Malcolm tugged as hard as he could, and Daniel popped out of the cage, a split second before the floor inside the cage slammed into the its own ceiling.

The trip was relatively uneventful after that, for they had food and water, in the brown bags. Of course, there was the hot sun, but other than that, everything was going well. And then, they finally reached the summit. A huge building stood before them, made of solid rock, with lava flowing down the sides, and gears engraved into the outside walls for decoration. They walked in, and there was the gem. It was blue like the sky, on a day with no clouds, blue like the ocean, the brightest blue possible. Malcolm's eyes widened, and he and Daniel walked towards it. It was then that they both fell down, down, down. And then they hit the floor.

4. THE DUNGEON OF PUZZLES

Malcolm got up and dusted himself off. Everything was in pain, but he could walk, and breathe. The air had been knocked out of him, but luckily, the contents of the bag of food on his back were intact. The air smelled misty, slightly smoky, and sort of stinky, like a flooded basement, like some water which had dried and left a strange smell in the air. "Daniel!" He called. There was no reply. "Daniel!" He said again, panic rising inside him.

"I'm over here!" A faint voice said. Malcolm stumbled over to the voice, before tripping over a large lump. "Ow!" Daniel groaned.

"Daniel! Are you alright?" Malcolm asked.

"I think so." Daniel replied. "This entire dungeon… I thought it was only a legend. If the legend is true, there should be some puzzles for us to solve. We will have to use our brains to escape. Suddenly, there was a whoosh, and light flooded the dungeon. Torches on the wall blazed, giving the dungeon an interesting glow. Malcolm looked up at where they had fallen from. It looked a long way up.

There was only one way to go, and that was forward. Malcolm walked ahead and was met by a pit, filled with insanely hot magma, with three stone pillars poking their heads out of the top of the wriggling, bubbling lava. The pillars were maybe five meters away from each other. There was also large wooden boards, about three to four meters long, on the far side of every pillar. However, this still left a two meter gap between the pillars. If you tried to jump, you would have to land perfectly on the narrow ledge and still somehow avoid falling into the lava. If you fall, you would be destined for a slow, agonizing death as the lava burned you alive.

"I have a plan." Malcolm announced, rather abruptly.

"I will go first." Daniel said, after Malcolm had explained his plan.

"No, I will!" Malcolm replied.

"No, trust me, I will go first!" Daniel insisted. Eventually, they decided that Malcolm could go first, because he was taller. They threw their bags filled with precious food and water across the lava pit, and they landed on the other side. Then, Malcolm, with Daniel's assistance, lied down between the end of the plank and the edge of the pit. Even from about a meter above the lava, and with his chestplate and tunic to protect him, Malcolm felt very exposed, like he was a pig being slowly cooked until tender under burning hot coals. Daniel stepped onto his back and Malcolm grunted with strain.

"Sorry!" Daniel said, sounding nervous.

"It's fine! Just be quick!" Malcolm replied, his core burning.

Daniel stepped between Malcolm's shoulder blades and hopped onto the plank. Malcolm sighed in relief, as Daniel carefully, one foot in front of the other walked over the plank.

"I'm on the pillar!" Daniel reported.

"Alright. Now, you know what to do, right?" Malcolm asked.

"Yes." Daniel replied.

Daniel kneeled down on the pillar and hugged Malcolm's waistline.

"Now pull up!" Malcolm shouted.

Daniel pulled until Malcolm was effectively doing a handstand on the edge of the pillar.

"Now let me down gently!" Malcolm yelled.

Daniel slowly lowered down Malcolm's legs. Malcolm was now doing a sort of bridge, arching his back. He collapsed, now lying at rest on the plank.

"Well, it worked…" Daniel said, smiling.

"Yes. Yes it did." Malcolm replied, with a tired grin on his face.

They continued in the same fashion on all the pillars, stopping for a rest after every painful human bridge process. Slowly but surely, they made it to the end. Daniel heaved Malcolm, who had been the bridge, up into a sitting position, and they looked at each other, smiling. The plan had worked! As Daniel basked in the glory of having completed the test, staring down the empty corridor ahead of them, there was a huge creak of heavy machinery and a gate crashed down a few meters in front of them. The dungeon wasn't finished yet.

Malcolm looked around for a way to escape the dungeon. Ahead, there were two black, metal letters. P and N. Then there was a ladder, which seemed like it was too high for them to use it. They tried to stand on each other's shoulders. The ladder was out of reach. Malcolm tried to jump up and grab the ladder. His fingers slipped, and he fell to the floor, landing awkwardly, before screaming in agony as his leg contorted in a horrible position. And then, there was a sickening crunch as his bone snapped.

Malcolm screamed and screamed and screamed. It felt like his leg was being burned up from the inside. He had never felt a pain that bad in his life. But Daniel acted quickly. His tribe were the best healers in the world. Everyone had been trained from a young age in healing and medicine. He looked in his bag, and took out a bottle. It was the specialty of the tribe, their pride and joy. It would be able to make Malcolm's broken leg good as new in a matter of minutes. But he would have to apply it fast. Already, Malcolm's leg was beginning to swell. Daniel began to gently rub the contents of the bottle onto the skin covering the break, before taking out some bandages, and applying them to the leg. The swelling was coming down already. *This is a job father would have been proud of.* He thought to himself.

"Wow!" Malcolm said. "What is that medicine?" The pain had abruptly stopped.

"That, my friend, is a secret!" Daniel replied with a twinkle in his eye.

"Why don't we climb on the letters to reach the ladder?" Daniel asked Malcolm, who was testing out his newly mended leg. It felt stiff, but he was getting used to it already. Or maybe it was just the stiffness wearing off.

"Malcolm!" Daniel said, trying to get his attention.

"What?" Malcolm said, his train of thought broken.

"I said, why don't we climb on the letters to reach the ladder?" Daniel shouted.

Malcolm's eyes brightened.

"That's a great idea!" He replied, excitedly.

So, they dragged the letters over and put the N over the P. They balanced perfectly, and sort of stuck together in a way, like magnets. Malcolm let Daniel climb on his back, and he stepped on the N. It held firm, and did not wobble. Daniel reached up as high as he could, and his right hand grasped the bottom rung. Then, he pulled himself up, grabbing the bottom rung with his left hand. Then, his arm muscles screaming at him to stop, he put his foot on the ladder. They had done it! Muscles burning, Daniel stuck out his foot for Malcolm to grab onto, and Malcolm jumped up and grabbed Daniel's leg. Daniel groaned but kept his leg stationary. Malcolm, who was holding the leg with his right arm, swung up his left arm and grabbed the bottom rung. Shifting his weight to his left arm, as Daniel sighed in relief, he let go of Daniel's leg, and quick as a flash, grabbed the bottom rung of the ladder with his right hand. He was now holding on with both of his hands, and Daniel helped him up. Malcolm put his feet on the rungs, and Daniel began to climb up, Malcolm following underneath. "The ladder ends here! There's a small outcrop with another ladder slightly to the the right!" Daniel called out.

"Keep going!" Malcolm replied.

At the outcrop, there was an O letter, and an E letter, exactly like the other letters.

"I guess we won't be needing these!" Daniel said, throwing them off the outcrop.

"Let's keep climbing." Malcolm said, looking up at the next ladder and wonder what would be at the top.

A dead end. That was what met the two men when they got to the top.

"That… that can't be!" Daniel cried, looking around for something, anything, which would tell them that everything was fine, that this was just a cruel trick the dungeon was playing. But there was nothing. Just a flat rock face, staring back at them. "I suppose it's back down again…" Malcolm said, trying and failing to keep the disappointment out of his voice.

"Yes. I suppose it is." Daniel replied, with a sad sigh.

The letters were lined up. "OPEN" is what it said. Malcolm smiled at the irony. He was also beginning to feel groggy and sluggish, suggesting that it was nighttime above ground. Malcolm was wondering whether he would ever even get to see sunlight again. Daniel was pounding at the gate, and looking in every nook and cranny for a way to escape. After a while, though, he gave up walking back to Malcolm, who was preparing their dinner. Water, dried fruit and meat. "It's no use," Daniel said, walking back to the main area. "We're going to be stuck here forever." He wasn't looking where he was going, and tripped on the N letter. "Dumb letters." He muttered, dusting himself off. However, Malcolm wasn't looking at Daniel. He was looking at the N letter, which was shaking. Then, the other letters began to shake, and then, they started to glow, yellow, orange, red, white hot, before they exploded.

When the smoke had cleared away, there was a crater in the ground, about three meters wide. Malcolm and

Daniel scrambled to their feet, for they had both been knocked over by the explosion. The crater wasn't very deep, or big, but still, it could help them to escape. Malcolm began examining the crater, looking for something to help them. His examining, though, was interrupted by the creak of heavy machinery. Malcolm turned his head and saw the gate slowly opening.

Malcolm and Daniel grabbed their belongings and ran towards the gate. Their chance at freedom was here, and they were going to take it. They sprinted under the gate, and stumbled into a hall of mirrors. A hall of mirrors. A colossal, gigantic, humongous hall of mirrors.

The ceilings were arched and incredibly high, made of stone the color of storm clouds. The room itself was massive, stretching out as far as the eye could see, making Malcolm feel incredibly small and insignificant. The mirrors were not framed, just upright rectangles, and very thin, to ensure that no one would attempt walking over the mirrors. The mirrors were also perfectly clean, not so much as a speck of dust on anything. Malcolm just stood still, his mouth slightly open, not sure where to start. The more fortunate children back home with rich, important parents had been invited to the castle to mirror halls. But none of them had been as big as the one which stood in front of them now. Malcolm had snuck in to the castle with his friends to steal scraps of food, when they had seen the mirrors. Malcolm himself had been the son of a poor farmer and a wife who did laundry in the village to buy clothes and other necessities. But Malcolm forced himself to stop thinking of home. He would never see it again if he and Daniel failed to deal with the current problem at hand. He glanced at Daniel, who was staring hard at the mirrors, as if he could drill a hole through everything if he concentrated hard enough. But this got Malcolm thinking. What if they tried to use brute force to get through the maze? It might just work. Malcolm took off his helmet, and began to charge at the nearest mirror, his arms in front of him, using the helmet as a battering ram. Then he crashed into the mirror, bouncing off and landing on the cold, hard floor. He rubbed his back as he walked over to the mirror. It wasn't broken. It hadn't been knocked over. And it wasn't dented. There wasn't even a single scratch. Malcolm then walked to the edges of the room. Could they squeeze through? No. They would get stuck. The gap was tiny. There was no way to avoid the task of going through the actual maze. Malcolm sighed. It was hopeless. He walked over to Daniel, who was still staring at the maze.

"Daniel! Hello!" Malcolm said as Daniel shook himself out of his trance.

"Yes?"

"I looked around. We have to just go through the maze. There is no other way."

"Alright."

So, taking their belongings, they took prepared themselves mentally for what was to come. Malcolm thought about asking Daniel if he had a plan, as Daniel thought the same thing the other way around. There was no clever plan this time. Only them and the mirrors.

"Ready?" Malcolm asked Daniel.

"I think so."

"Alright. Then, let's go."

They grabbed their bags, and took a step into the hall of mirrors. Instantly, Malcolm was met by several reflections of himself and Daniel. It was all so confusing. A deep heat began to rise in Malcolm. Not exactly anger, but more... determination. Malcolm began to run. Dragging Daniel behind him, feeling his way around for openings to keep going, with just one goal in mind. Get to the end of the maze.

"Malcolm, what are you doing?" Daniel yelled, as he was being dragged around.

"I'm getting us out of here!" Malcolm replied. He eliminated the mirrors from his mind. He pictured the walls as dense foliage in the forests in England, playing with his friends, and then, when he was fourteen, killing a massive boar with his knife. He had lost his sense of time, but suddenly, they stumbled out into an opening. They saw the gem on a pedestal, right in front of them. They were safe. They had the gem. And they were tired, beads of sweat running down their cheeks. But they were safe. And finally, they had done it. They had escaped from the dungeon.

Daniel grabbed the gem. It was warm to the touch, and it smelled sweet, like flowers on a hot summer day.

"Come on!" Daniel said to Malcolm, helping him up. They jumped over the spot where they had dropped into the dungeon at the beginning of this whole thing. The floor didn't open, but, better be safe than sorry. They stepped out into the open, the fresh air hitting them. It was one of the best feelings in the world after being cooped up underground for so long. They both inhaled, taking a moment to relish their freedom. Then they set off on the long journey back to bandit village.

5. A WAR BEGINS

They dodged the cage trap this time, and no goblins bothered them. The sun was still hot as always, but, eventually, they made it back to village. People were buzzing around, washing clothes, planting seeds, cooking, playing, and talking. Meanwhile, Malcolm and Daniel hid behind a wide tree.

"Should we go?" Malcolm whispered.

"It's now or never." Daniel replied. They sprinted into the village.

There was an awkward silence.

"Seize them!" A man with a deep voice screamed, as some guards ran towards them. It was Daniel's father. Quickly, Daniel opened his bag and rummaged through it, guiding his hands towards the warmth that the gem gave off. Soon, he found it, and grabbed it, holding it up.

"We have found the Gem of Life!" He cried, as the guards closed in.

Everyone froze.

"The Gem of Life?" Daniel's father asked, incredulously. People began to peek out of their houses until everyone in the entire village was surrounding the guards, Daniel's father, Malcolm, and Daniel.

"Yes, father," Daniel replied, trying to stay calm.

"Bring in Diego!" Daniel's father yelled.

"Diego?" One of the guards asked. "Are you sure?"

"I heard he's under intensive care!" Another guard said.

"Yes, I know!" Daniel's father replied. "But bring him in!"

"Who's Diego?" Malcolm whispered to Daniel.

"You'll see," Daniel said, grimacing. "You'll see."

Diego was brought in on a stretcher. Every few seconds he began to shake, screaming in pain.

"Torture flu." Daniel told Malcolm. "It's in the name, basically. Diego isn't screaming because he's crazy. He's screaming because he's actually in pain. We do have a cure, but it takes a very long time to take action."

"Silence!" Daniel's father yelled. "If they can cure Diego with the gem, then, all punishments against them will be lifted."

"And Malcolm will be a member of the village. Father, it is in the Scroll of the Ancients. You must let Malcolm be a member."

"If this works." Daniel's father cut in. Malcolm looked at Diego. He looked like he may have once been handsome. But he had a sort of gray color. He looked incurable. For the first time in a while, Malcolm began to doubt. Would this work? What would happen to him if it didn't? He had no idea.

"Begin!" Daniel's father yelled. Malcolm held the gem over Diego, waving it around. *Please. Just do whatever you're supposed to be doing.* Malcolm thought to the gem. After a while, he handed it to Daniel, who set the gem on Diego's stomach. Diego kept shaking. The gem had done nothing.

"Take them." Daniel's father said. Someone yawned.

"Daddy yawned!" A small child cried. "Daddy yawned!"

"Why is everyone looking at me? Why am I on this stretcher? Why is there a gem on me?" Diego asked.

"Daddy!" The child yelled, running up to Diego.

"He… he's cured!" Said a lady who was running next to the child to Diego. They all came together in an embrace.

"I was never sick!" Diego said, standing up, setting the gem down and wrapping his arms tighter around the lady and child, while grinning and showing teeth which were suddenly pearly white.

"You had Torture flu." The lady said.

"Torture flu?" Diego asked, his smile wiped from his face.

"Yes. They cured you with the Gem of Life," the lady replied, tears flowing like rivers down her cheeks.

"Why does Diego have no memory of his sickness?" Malcolm whispered.

"It is normal with survivors of Torture flu."

"Oh."

"I think we can safely say that the gem is real. Wouldn't you agree?" Daniel asked his father.

"I suppose."

"So then, let Malcolm vote."

Daniel's father hesitated. "I… I can't."

"You must." Daniel replied, and his father's face hardened.

"I won't."

"Let him vote!" Someone chanted. It was the lady, who was no doubt Diego's wife.

"Let him vote!" Diego chanted. Then their child started to chant. More and more people started to take up the chant, until everyone except the guards and Daniel's father was chanting.

"Let him vote! Let him vote! Let him vote!"

"Enough!" The piercing, angry scream of Daniel's furious father cut through the enthusiastic chant like a hot knife through butter.

"Malcolm will vote!" He yelled, and everyone cheered. Malcolm ran up to the voting containers, and picked up a green leaf. He waited until everyone was looking. And he dropped the leaf into the container.

"583 to 584!" He roared.

"583 to 584!" The crowd roared back.

"We will rebel!" He roared. The crowd said nothing.

"We will rebel!" He roared again. Still, no reaction. Out of the corner of his eye, he saw Daniel pointing frantically at him and making spinning gestures with his hands. Malcolm got the idea. He spun on his heel and saw a man with a black cloak, black boots, black pants, black everything. Even his eyes and shoulder length hair were dark black. In contrast to that, he had pale skin, and looked like he was in his late thirties. He was maybe a little less than six feet tall.

"Oh, my apologies. I forgot to introduce myself. How silly of me!" The man said, with a strong, posh, British accent. "My name is Ervarath, and I have come to kill you all."

Ervarath then proceeded to run off into the jungle. "Where is he going?" Malcolm wondered aloud. No one answered. But now, slowly, people began to pull themselves together, running to the armory hut or their houses for weapons, food, and other useful items. Daniel did the same. And then there was Malcolm. What was he supposed to do? He decided to grab some food. But where could he find food? And what was Ervarath doing? An incredibly quiet whooshing sound forced him to look up. No one else had heard it. But he had. A giant fireball, about ten meters wide, was flying through the sky. And it was heading straight towards them.

"Run!" He screamed. "Run for your lives! Run!" He began to sprint through the village, screaming the same words again and again, so everyone could hear. "Run!" Everyone ran, with their odd bags, weapons, and armor. Malcolm glanced up at the sky. The fireball had been high in the sky when he had seen it. Now it was a lot closer. They had some time. Maybe thirty seconds now. He estimated that they had to be at least one hundred meters away from the fireball when it hit. And then it happened. One second he was running. The next second, boom! The sound rattled his eardrums. Then the sound of crackling as the village began to burn.

"How did they escape?" Ervarath asked his top minion, who was a red goblin just like all the other minions. His name was Grabble, and he hoped that he wouldn't get punished. He knew about Ervarath's fiery temper.

"Well?" Ervarath asked again, raising his voice.

"I'm not sure, master," he replied carefully, his three eyes focusing on his feet. "I suspect it may be the knight."

"What knight?" Ervarath asked, gingerly sipping some fresh pineapple juice that was in a crystal glass by his side.

"We don't know too much about him. But he and his friend are causing problems. They also seem to be responsible for the deaths of three minions we sent to intercept them on their quest for the Gem of Life. Ervarath growled, struggling to contain his fury.

"Kill them," he said.

6. A NEW BEGINNING

Everyone worked together to build a shelter that night. A few people had brought axes, which they used to chop down five huge sixty meter trees. They then cut the trees to make parts for a huge shelter. But how would they build the shelter? Everyone began to argue.

"Why don't we build a treehouse?" A man asked.

"A treehouse?"

"Do you think this is just for fun?" A man holding a spear asked. "No! One small mistake might lead to the deaths of us all!" He continued, angrily.

"But the treehouse would protect us from ground threats!"

"And if Ervarath's army chop down the tree in the night?"

"We can have some people keeping watch in shifts!"

In the end, it was decided. The treehouse would be made. Since there were over one thousand people that needed to fit in the treehouse, the floor would be supported by four massive trees. The best climbers in the village were selected to climb the tree, with a small, light bag slung over their shoulder containing a few planks. One climber carried nails, screws, and a rope ladder in his bag. Soon the climbers were on a large, low, branch, about ten meters up, and a small floor was built. Next, the rope ladder was attached to the floor, and more people climbed up the tree. After that, a small search team went out to the remains of the village to salvage what was left. Malcolm was in the team, which consisted of about twenty people. Each member had an axe for self defense and practical uses. They also had a backpack and a large cloth sack to carry more things. On the way back, Malcolm prepared himself for what he might see. Would he see any dead bodies? Though he might have killed people before, they were his enemies. They were trying to kill him! This would be different. These people were his allies. He knew there had been a few losses. Over the past day, he had seen some people quietly mourning their dead relatives. Would he see the charred, blackened, body of some random person? He didn't know. But the trip to the village was brief, and he soon arrived there along with the rest of the team, which stopped his train of thought. "Should we split up?" A man asked.

"Sure. Why don't we go in teams of two?" A short, stocky woman replied. Everyone agreed, and Malcolm was paired with a young man with very short hair and dark skin. Each pair was assigned to a certain area of the village, and Malcolm had a chance to see the village from a different angle, rather than from his cage. He could see a large, charred, ball of rock close to the center of the village. It was huge, perhaps fifty meters across. It was no doubt the fireball. The only way you could fire something that large would probably use magic. Malcolm wondered if Ervarath was a powerful magician, but he shrugged the thought aside. It was an unpleasant, worrying, ugly thought. He didn't like those kinds of thoughts. Malcolm went back to the task at hand, which was going inside all of the houses in the area, taking anything useful with them. Their bags were almost full with items when they heard a man scream in pain.

Malcolm ran out of the house, drawing his sword. It slid out with the same metallic ring it always made. Malcolm's partner, who was called Jose, drew his dagger. They ran toward the scream, and saw a man with black, shoulder length hair with a dart in his leg. He looked pale and lifeless, and he was lying in front of a house. Then Malcolm looked the other way, and saw ten red goblins holding blowguns. They were all pointing at him.

The goblins blew, and the darts flew out of the barrel of the gun. Malcolm dived to his left, and the dart flew into the wall of the house that he had been standing in front of. Then he scrambled away before the goblins could release another volley of deadly darts. He risked a peek around the house. Now the goblins were aiming at the injured man! He wasn't screaming anymore. Was he dead? Malcolm couldn't just leave him to die there. He had to do something! He scurried over and dragged away the injured man.

"It's all right. It's going to be alright," Malcolm said in his most reassuring voice. The man groaned in reply. But he wondered if he had just uttered a lie. He didn't know how to heal! Where was everyone else? Malcolm decided to take matters into his own hands. He began by closely examining the wound. The dart was embedded deep into the man's quadriceps. But what was he supposed to do?

"Belt," the man said. "Heal." The words sounded like a shoe scraping against gravel.

Malcolm looked around the man's waist. Then he saw the small leather pouch. It was simple and worn, the opening flaps being held together by two buttons. Malcolm gently opened the pouch.

"Leave it to us," said a voice, before Malcolm could take out the contents of the pouch. It was the short lady who had suggested the pairs. She had come with her partner, a tall, thin woman with ink black, straight, hair. Malcolm was happy to. A part of him wanted to stay by the injured man's side, but he had more important matters to attend to, such as the threat of imminent death because of the goblins. Surely they were advancing! How close were they? Leaving the injured man with the two women, he ran to the side of the house. The goblins were close. Too close. He couldn't safely approach, though, as he would be right in the line of fire. But then a man crept out behind the goblins. Jose! He gave Malcolm a nervous smile. Then he leapt into the air and, using his dagger, slashed and stabbed at the goblins. He moved like lightning, his movement abrupt and quick. Before Malcolm could even blink, two goblins lay dead. This was his chance. He ran forward, muscles pumping. Malcolm spun, holding out his sword. Three goblins were cut in half from the torso, screaming in agony. Jose stabbed, sunlight glinting off his blade, making it look like a deadly, metallic, snake. A goblin went down, clutching his stomach. But the remaining four goblins were beginning to fight back. A deadly dart flew through the air, coming towards Malcolm. He ducked just in time. Malcolm lunged desperately, trying to gain the upper hand. His sword cut deep into the leg of his target. The goblin hopped away on his good leg, squealing. Three goblins left to go. Jose stabbed twice, his attacks accurate and fatal. Two goblins went down. The remaining goblin had the sense to scurry away. Malcolm stumbled over back to the house. Some color was returning to the injured man's face, and by now everyone was by his side.

"Thank you for saving my life," he said to Malcolm. "I would have died without your help. I am Joao."

"No problem. I'm glad you're alright," Malcolm replied. Jose ran up to them holding a crude crutch of sorts. He gave it to Joao, who gratefully took it. Joao carefully stood up, and gathered his belongings, which had either fallen off him or been removed to increase his comfort.

"What did we manage to find?" Someone asked. People took off their bags and began to show what they had found. Weapons, food, clothes, medicine, and things like nails, hammers, rope, and hinges for doors.

"We should get the remains of the houses sometime. It could really help us build our shelter." Jose said. Everyone agreed, happy with what they had found. Then they started the way back home.

"Sir, they got away again," Grabble said.

"They what?" Ervarath replied, flying into a rage.

"We sent ten of our best poison dart minions to ambush them while they were trying to salvage materials. We hit one man, but he survived. All but one of our troops were killed."

"Grabble, you better find a way to eliminate this knight, or I will kill you in the most painful way I can think of." Ervarath said, his voice dangerously calm.

"Yes, sir."

By the time they got back, the treehouse was almost done. The sun was beginning to set, casting its bright oranges, yellows, reds, and pinks over the rainforest. Malcolm couldn't help but smile to himself. He saw Daniel studying a map with his father and discussing something. Malcolm called out to him and Daniel turned around with a smile on his face.

"Malcolm! What did you find?"

"Many tools and weapons. However, there are still valuable items left. We were ambushed by some of Ervarath's minions. They had blowguns."

"Any casualties?" Daniel asked.

"No." Malcolm replied. "But Joao was injured."

Daniel's father muttered something under his breath. Daniel ignored him.

"Our treehouse is almost done. We also have food and water covered. We sent a large team to fish for the whole day and we are close to a having a fish for every person. We are currently boiling the water to clean it."

"Sounds good," Malcolm replied. Daniel opened his mouth, then saw something.

"Not there! How many times do I have to tell you, Lucas? That's not where the support beam goes!" Daniel yelled while running towards the treehouse. Daniel's father awkwardly cleared his throat.

"We have never introduced ourselves to each other. We must all work together to beat Ervarath. I am Antonio."

"I am Malcolm."

With that, Antonio walked away and lifted a small log, carefully placing it on a wooden platform, which was attached to a rope that ran over a pulley perched on the treehouse floor. The world was now bathed in a dreamy shade of orange coming from the setting sun. A parrot squawked as it flew over the trees. Things were going well. But not for long.

The dark jungle was silent save for the occasional animal noise. The minion pulled out his axe, and his five partners followed suit. Then they began to hack at the tree trunk.

Daniel awoke to the sound of metal hitting wood. He sat up, rubbing the sleep out of his eyes. Malcolm snored on the mattress next to him, his tangled, messy brown hair draped over his pillow. Daniel got up and grabbed a spear, tiptoeing to the nearest ladder. It was folded up on the floorboards. Daniel pushed it down, and it unraveled until the bottom was nearly touching the damp jungle floor. The top was bolted to the floorboards. Daniel carefully climbed down. When he got near the bottom of the ladder, he hopped down, landing soundlessly on the jungle floor. The minions took no notice of him, continuing to swing their axes at the tree. Daniel sprang into action. The minions were taken by surprise, and they clumsily swung their axes in a fruitless attempt to defend themselves. It was over quickly. They were no match for Daniel and his spear. He wiped its tip with a leaf, and climbed back up the ladder. Then he dropped the spear on the floor and went back to sleep, like nothing had happened.

Ervarath admired Grabble's charred body. He had been useless anyway. His new top minion was much better. Grabble had been burned alive, but Ervarath thought it wasn't painful enough. Watching Grabble scream in agony had still been fun, though. Maybe he would try something different next time.

Jose dragged himself through the jungle. They were heading to their first battle. He and about one hundred other volunteers were trying to get to Ervarath's castle, and Jose knew where it was. Everyone did. Ervarath had told them when he saw them as allies, but that wasn't the case anymore. They were armed with whatever they could find, such as slings, spears, daggers, axes, swords, bows and arrows, and maces. Those who couldn't get their hands on a weapon simply carried rocks or sharpened sticks. Jose knew they were close, and a shiver ran down his spine. And his muscles tensed in anticipation. Suddenly, the trees fell away to show a large clearing. The battleground. Then the castle came into view.

Ervarath almost spat out his food when he saw the advancing army. He got out of his chair and screamed to no one in particular,
"We need a strong resistance! Quick!"

The goblins came out of the castle like a swarm of angry red bees. They had all sorts of weapons. They shrieked a battle cry as they charged at their enemies, faces angry and determined. Jose and the other volunteers roared and hurled rocks, spears, and sticks at the opposition. Most of the projectiles hit their targets, making the minions stumble, knocking them out, or injuring or killing them. Jose saw his friend Pedro leap into the oncoming crowd of minions, swinging his axe around him, killing anyone who got near him. A minion came towards him and he stabbed it with his dagger. Three more came at him and he casually impaled them in three quick movements. Meanwhile, Pedro stood with countless dead minions lying around him. Not a single minion even tried to come close to him. The minions were no match for the skillful bandits. Suddenly, there was a roar of flames that came from the sky. Jose looked up to see the fireball coming towards him.

Malcolm was talking with Daniel when he heard an explosion which rattled his eardrums. Startled, they both looked in the direction of the explosion. There was a large column of smoke and flames coming up into the sky, high above the jungle trees.
"Jose…" Malcolm breathed.

Everyone wore a solemn, sad look on their faces, mourning the deaths of the 100 volunteers who had died. There was silence apart from the sounds of the jungle. The rustling leaves of the trees, a squeal or growl from an animal. The fire crackled and snapped, illuminating the world around it in various shades of orange and red. The sky was black like coal, and a breeze blew. There were no survivors. Antonio cleared his throat and began to speak.

"As you all know, Ervarath launched another fireball at our brave army. They had no chance. But we can't let ourselves sit here and wait for Ervarath to pick us off. It is clear he has some sort of machine, but from now on, we will watch the sky. Ervarath will pay for what he has done to us!" The crowd roared in approval, their anger towards Ervarath fueling their morale. "He will pay!" Antonio yelled.

The next day, a new team set off, following the same path the first volunteers had taken. This time, there were twice as many people, and in the middle of the army, ten men watched the sky. They had all threats covered. Soon, they reached the castle, and a flow of red came out of its doors like a sea of blood. It was Ervarath's minions. There were so many. Thousands. The bandits leapt into action, skillfully fighting. There were a few casualties on their side, but most of the deaths were on Ervarath's side. Minions fell like dominos. It was carnage. It was chaos. The air was filled with the sounds of yelling and metal clanging.

"Hey!" A man called. "Hey!" He was surrounded by bandits, who were defending him as best as could. He was one of the fireball watchers, and he was pointing at the sky. There was a fireball, still very high in the air. It took very little time for all the bandits to notice, and soon they were running for their lives into the trees surrounding the battleground. The minions, too, had noticed the fireball, and they were pointing at the sky and squealing while they ran away, to the safety of Ervarath's castle. There was a second of complete silence. Then, an explosion which rattled the eardrums of Malcolm and Daniel, who were standing on the balcony at the highest part of the treehouse, watching the fight from afar. A huge cloud of smoke floated into the sky, and the fireball became visible. It roared with flames for a few minutes before they died out, as there was nothing for them to catch on to.

"Pack up," Antonio said, as he walked onto the balcony. "We're going to war."

Ervarath's castle was a little bit southwest from the middle of the map, which lay on the damp jungle ground as Antonio explained the plan. The treehouse was about thirty kilometers south from the castle. 150 men attentively listened to Antonio as he explained the plan, which was to advance along the flanks. The left group would help fight Ervarath and his minions, while the right would arc around the castle, to surprise the enemy. Daniel and Malcolm were on the right side, and Antonio was leading. Joao, who had healed, was at the left side. A trusted friend of Antonio was leading the left. After everyone knew what to do, they set off at dawn the next day. The push was uneventful, until they got news from the left side. The news came in the form of a brightly colored parrot, which fluttered over to Malcolm while he and his group set up camp. There was a piece of paper tied to its leg. Someone had scrawled a few sentences on it.

We have reached Ervarath's castle, and joined the original army. We surrounded the castle, and besieged it. The minions are fighting back, though, and we are struggling to hold them off. We also captured a minion, who told us that Ervarath has decided to flee to a hut up north. We suggest that you go look for that hut, but be warned. The minion also told us that Ervarath hired a Mongol Assassin.

Malcolm knew about Mongol Assassins. They were the best archers in the world. They could hit an ant from a mile away. He showed the note to Antonio and Daniel. Antonio drew a crude copy of a map on the back of the note, with the words,

Understood. Can you make a mark around where the hut is?

With that, all 75 bandits ate a simple dinner, and went to sleep. Well, most of them, anyway.

Malcolm couldn't sleep. He had a feeling, deep down in his heart, that something was about to go horribly wrong. He couldn't make the feeling go away, it just stayed there, persistent. He tossed and turned, trying, and failing, to make himself comfortable. Nothing worked. The feeling was like anxiety. Eventually, after a couple of hours, Malcolm dozed off. But when he woke up the next morning, the feeling was still there.

They marched on and on, as they now knew where the hut was. For once Malcolm had a chance to observe the jungle, as the march was silent and dreary. He noticed how thick the jungle air was. It was like honey, and that was probably why it felt so difficult for Malcolm to walk for long periods of time. The sun began to set, and he tingled in anticipation. They couldn't be more than a kilometer away. They went around a bend in the extremely narrow path, and they saw it. It was a very small hut in a large clearing, with a rocky hill next to it. The hill was about ten meters high, and there were several scraggly bushes in various crevices on the hill. One of the bigger, thicker bushes rustled in the nonexistent breeze, and Malcolm narrowed his eyes. He glanced at Daniel, who was bouncing on the balls of his feet with his eyes closed, taking deep breaths. Antonio was standing still. He turned his head towards Malcolm, then uttered a single word.

"Go." They advanced, and Malcolm kicked down the light wooden door.

Ervarath was sitting at a table in his hut, studying a map. He saw Malcolm, sword drawn, he saw Antonio, his sharp dagger in hand, and he saw Daniel, who stood in the doorway, his dagger also ready. Ervarath didn't seem to be startled. Almost like he was expecting them.

"Stay still and cooperate." Antonio said. Suddenly there was a smack of a longbow string releasing, and the sound of Daniel crying out in pain.

Antonio ran outside and looked around for whoever had hit his son. Sure enough, he saw a figure running out of the bush that had been his cover. The Mongolian Assassin. Antonio quickly snatched up a rock as big as an apple near the foot of the rocky hill, and lobbed it high into the air. It smashed into the Assassin's head with a crack. But suddenly, Malcolm sensed something. Danger. Behind him. He spun around to see Ervarath charging at him, brandishing a large spear. It would be very hard to win this fight. The length of the spear would give Ervarath an advantage. Then, Malcolm saw a pile of pebbles out of the corner of his eye. He had an idea. He sidestepped a few times, till he was in front of the pile of pebbles. Ervarath didn't notice it. A fatal mistake. He tripped over the pile, landing on his stomach with his hands sprawled out in front of him and the spear just out of his reach. Malcolm got ready for the final blow. He hacked down to cut off Ervarath's neck. But stopped.

"I should kill you right now," he spat. "It's what you deserve. But…"

He picked up the spear and threw it into the jungle. "One move, you're dead," Malcolm warned. Then he turned to Daniel.

"There's no pulse… There's no pulse," Antonio was muttering to himself. He started to sob quietly. Malcolm paused, trying to understand what he had heard. Then he did. Malcolm staggered. It couldn't be. Daniel, his companion, his ally, his friend… dead? A fiery rage ripped free of its chains deep in Malcolm's heart. His raw emotions came out in the forms of screams and tears. He had to help Daniel. Revive him. But how?

7. THE IMPORTANT FRUIT

They rushed through the jungle. Daniel was not dead. In a way. He lay, in a vegetative state, on a makeshift stretcher. At least they had done their job. Ervarath's hands were firmly tied and the minions back at Ervarath's castle had surrendered. However, there was now a new problem at hand. Daniel. The arrow's tip had been coated with poison and it had pierced Daniel's chest. He didn't have much time, five days at best. But the Gem of Life would surely work. All they had to do is get back to the treehouse safely, and heal Daniel. The journey back was easy. The goblins had returned to normal, no longer serving Ervarath and causing chaos and destruction. They arrived at the treehouse in less than two days. As soon as they arrived, they went up to the treehouse and got the Gem of Life. Every minute counted. They grabbed it from its place and put it on Daniel's chest and waited.

And waited. Nothing was happening. They moved it around. They rubbed it. Still, nothing happened. Daniel's breath was fainter than ever. Nothing was working.

"What was in the poison?" Malcolm ran to Ervarath and shouted.

"The poison is special," Ervarath replied calmly. "The Gem of Life won't work! But I will tell you what will. Soon," he said.

Antonio spoke about what had happened, until the time came to decide what to do with Ervarath.

"Kill him! After all he has done, it is what he deserves!" Some people said.

"No! Let him live! We are a tribe of life and healing! Give him another chance!" Others said. Eventually it was decided. Ervarath would live, but he would do work for the rest of his life. But what about Daniel?

"Ervarath! What about my son? Is there an antidote to the poison on the arrow?" Antonio asked.

"Yes," Ervarath replied. "But I will only tell you if you heal your brother. He is my best friend. All I wanted to do was cure him. But even that I couldn't do. I wish it hadn't been this complicated. I wish that so many people didn't have to die."

"We will." Antonio replied. "I was working with you before to save my brother! But you have to tell us what to do to save my son."

"The antidote is the juice of a special fruit. The fruit is very rare, with a consistency similar to that of a mango. It is bright green, and found on a tree with a purple trunk." Ervarath said.

Malcolm had no other choice but to go off and find the fruit. He and a large group of people took food and water, and left the village. They would spread out, looking for the unmistakable purple trees that the fruits grew on. The others would stay back at base, trying experimental healing concoctions made of mysterious, exotic ingredients. Malcolm was sure that someone would be attacked by some horrible creature, as they would be alone, something which would surely attract the Amazonian wildlife. On top of that, Daniel had less than three days. The odds were not looking good. However, this did not demotivate Malcolm. He had to try. He had to try for Daniel.

Malcolm felt a sense of urgency and importance as he trudged through the jungle. He still felt relatively fresh, as he had set off a few hours ago. He stepped on a strange, curly, branch, expecting a soothing crack. Instead, the branch hissed and reared up at him. A snake! Malcolm quickly drew his sword, faking a jab, and then slashing his sword in a swift, flowing, movement. The snake fell to the ground, separated into two parts, and a bead of sweat ran down Malcolm's cheek. He had no time to celebrate his victory, though. He had to find the fruit before Daniel's situation became worse and worse. Sheathing his sword, he carried on through his haphazard, rather desperate path through the jungle. Malcolm kept at it, forcing any negative thoughts or feelings out of his troubled mind, until the inky blackness of the night wrapped its dark arms around the jungle and held tight.

Malcolm packed up his tent and items at the crack of dawn the next day, eager to carry on with his search for the tree. The sun stretched its pale yellow tip over the horizon, and Malcolm wondered if anyone else had found the tree yet, and he hoped that was the case. The rule was that if anyone found the fruit, they were to report back to base immediately. Upon their arrival, some sort of whistle or horn would be blown, signaling for the searchers to return. The same whistle or horn would be blown if someone found a solution with their strange concoctions. But, Daniel would now have less than two days to live, and Malcolm was feeling very tired. Left alone
with himself, his thoughts, and the jungle the day before, Malcolm had almost subconsciously pushed himself too far. It was also peculiar, he thought, how the jungle seemed to suck the life, the energy, right out of you. But that didn't matter. Right now, his needs weren't important. Daniel's were. But Malcolm's main obstacle in this search for the fruit would mostly be himself, he figured. His own physical health. Even now that was a problem. Suddenly, Malcolm's limbs were getting heavier and heavier. He

was struggling to keep moving. He was struggling to stay standing. He slumped to the floor.

Pain. All Malcolm could feel was pain. He opened his eyes, to see that he was still in the jungle. The sun had barely moved from its spot in the sky before he had collapsed, but already the jungle scavengers had prepared to enjoy a large feast. Malcolm sat up and wiped the oily maggots and the ants, with their many legs and sharp mandibles, off his body. He tried to stand up, but failed. Then, out of his peripheral vision, he saw a purple shape. Could it be? He crawled towards it on all fours. Sure enough, the tree was dotted with bright green fruits. Malcolm slumped against the tree, trying to use his body weight to his advantage, and three of the fruits fell into Malcolm's lap. The fruits seemed to radiate all things positive. They seemed to scream healing and growth. And that's when Malcolm's tired, overworked brain made a connection it should have made a day or two before. Food. Water. That was why Malcolm was in this situation! He had been so busy thinking about things that he hadn't had time for one of the most vital things for survival. Malcolm desperately reached into the light bag on his back. He took out a flask, some pecan nuts, and some acai berries. He poured water into his mouth, which felt like sandpaper now that Malcolm, under the shade of the special tree, had come to his senses. His grateful body gulped the water down, and Malcolm threw a handful of acai berries and pecan nuts into his mouth. His body screamed for more, and Malcolm obliged. It took a long time for him to feel remotely normal again. He lay down on the jungle floor, and decided to have a short, perhaps fifteen minute nap, to prepare himself for the journey back to base. Soon, he drifted into a light, peaceful sleep.

Malcolm woke up. He felt ready, rested. He took a few deep breaths, and made sure that he had all of his stuff. The sun's point in the sky indicated that it was a little past noon. Good. That meant that Malcolm had around a day and a half to get back to the village. He let his desire, his determination, to save his friend take over, and he began to run. He held his flask in one hand, his light shoes soundlessly pounding the jungle floor. He got into a rhythm, and lost track of time, until the sun began to fall towards the horizon, bathing the jungle in brilliant pinks and yellows and oranges and reds, encouraging the night to take over.

Malcolm forced himself to wake up early the next morning. He packed up his tent, had a quick breakfast of water and a few handfuls of nuts and berries, and went on his way. He continued through the jungle at the same pace as the day before, and a couple of hours after he had set off, he burst into a clearing. Relief flooded over Malcolm. There was a man sitting on the ground with a horn. Malcolm ran up to him, eagerly showing what he had found. The man blew into the horn, and people began to emerge out of the treehouse, climbing down the ladders.

"See that hut over there?" The man with the horn asked, pointing in the direction of a hut. Malcolm nodded. "That's where Daniel is." Malcolm made his way over to where the man was pointing, taking the fruits out of his bag. He gently pushed some ropes covering the entrance to the side, and stepped in.

The hut was simple and smelled of death. Inside, Daniel was lying on a mattress. He was incredibly pale, and his skin was stretched over his bones. He looked like a skeleton. Antonio was sitting on a stool right next to Daniel, staring blankly at the wall. Malcolm carefully tapped him on the shoulder, and Antonio sharply turned his head.

"Malcolm! You have no idea how happy I am to see you! I just hope this works," he said, trying his best to smile.

"How do we use the fruit? Malcolm asked. Antonio pointed at a mortar and pestle on the floor right next to him.

"We don't even know if Daniel is alive or not," Antonio said sadly.

"Well, we have to try," Malcolm said. He put one of the fruits into the mortar and used the pestle to pound it until all of its juices were out. Then, Malcolm took the now juiceless fruit out of the mortar and set it down, along with the pestle. He opened Daniel's jaws and pretended to pour the juices in. A glance at Antonio, who nodded, told Malcolm that he was doing the right thing.

"Would you like to do this?" Malcolm asked.

"No, you should. After all, you found the fruits," Antonio said. Malcolm carefully poured the juices into Daniel's mouth. Nothing happened for a few agonizingly long minutes. All the bandits were holding their breath. Then Daniel's eyes sprang open.

EPILOGUE

The sea breeze blew, as Malcolm watched the bandits wave goodbye. Soon, they were all but a speck. He felt sad that he had to leave, but he was excited to return home too. He gave the two remaining fruits to Luis, Rafaela, and the other villagers. England had also decided to help expand the bandits' treehouse and make sure that all the tribes and villages had the resources they needed to do everything they wanted, and live in peace. When he returned to England to his family, Malcolm was going to share all the things he had experienced, found, and learned. Now, he was on an English ship which was taking him home. He had learned a lot during his time with Daniel and the bandits, his adventures in the jungle, and even through his battles with Everath; and he would never forget all that had happened to him. But as the waves gently rocked the ship, and Malcolm drifted farther and farther away from his life for the past year, he vowed that this was not over. He would someday return.

ABOUT THE AUTHOR

Ari Cumbusyan was born in 2007 in New York City, grew up in London until the age of 6, and then, moved to Zurich where he currently attends Fifth Grade at Zurich International School. He likes football, video games, reading, running, skiing, eating good food, playing the guitar, making jokes, and hanging out with friends.